The Adventures of the Owl and the Pussycat

written by Coral Rumble

illustrated by Charlotte Cooke

PaRragon

Bath • New York • Singapore • Hong Kong • Cologne • Delhi
Melbourne • Amsterdam • Johannesburg • Shenzhen

The Owl and the Pussycat went to sea
In a box on the living room floor,
They sailed away for a year and a day
And these are the things that they saw...

A wiggly, squiggly eel
Dancing with a cheerful seal,

A bottle bobbing by
With a treasure map inside,

A shark in a spin
With a cat on his fin,

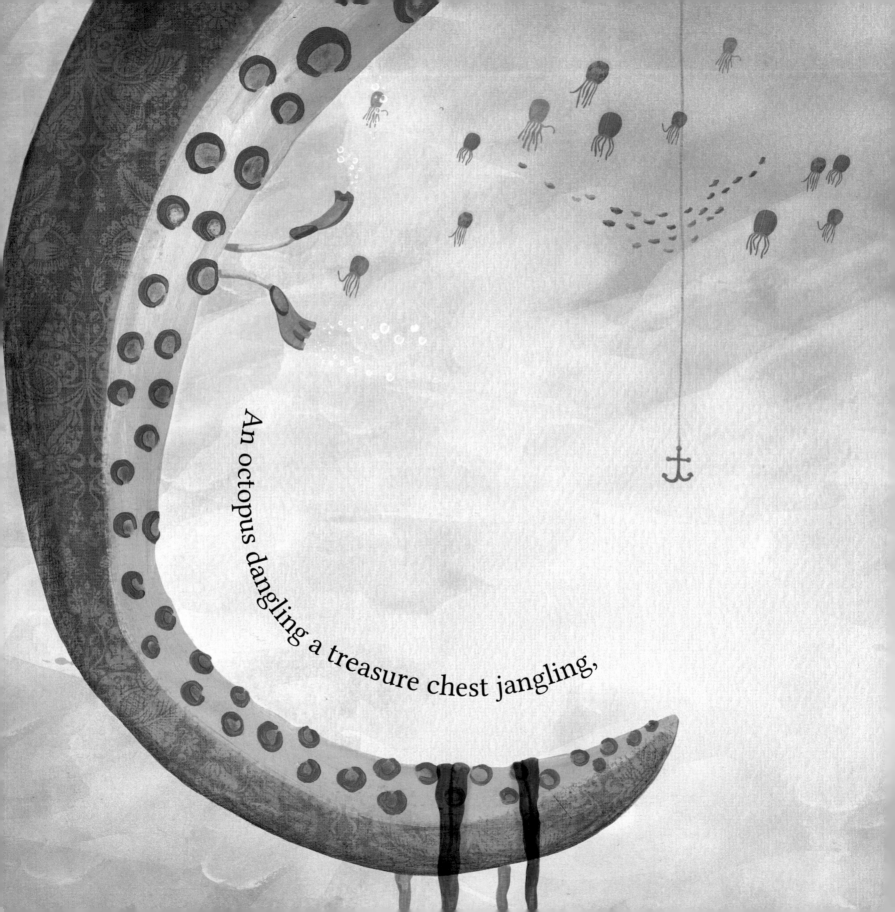

An octopus dangling a treasure chest jangling,

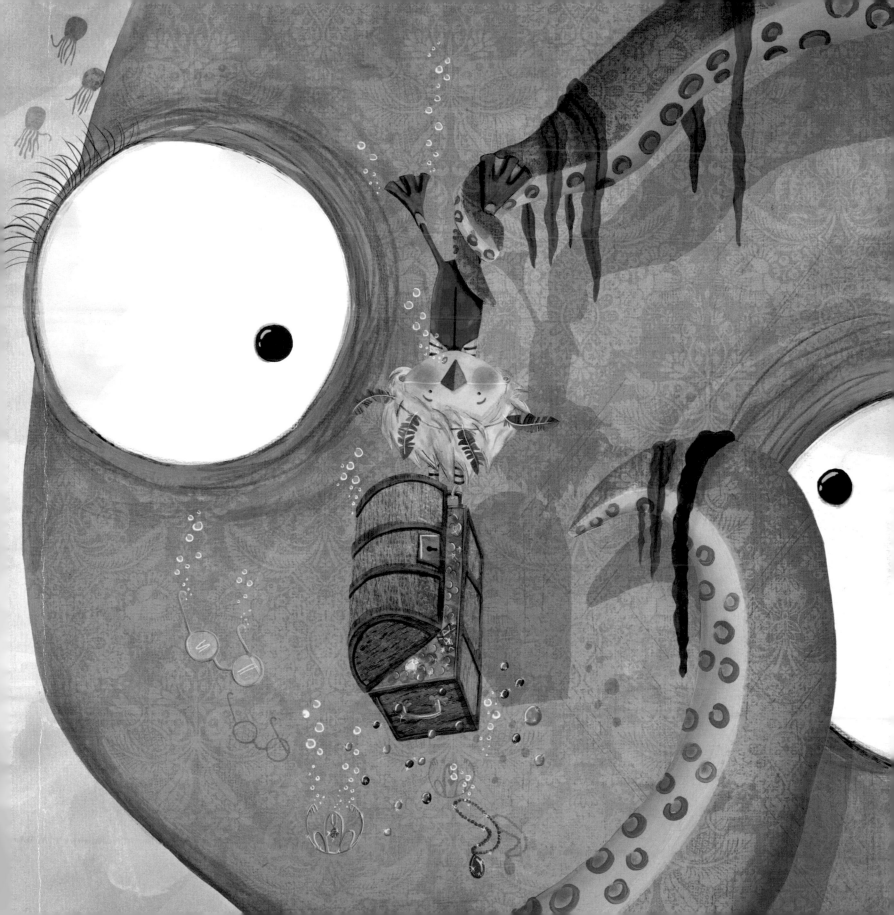

A clownfish playing the flute

In a bow tie and a suit,

A starfish in the sun,

A naughty seagull
having fun,

A lobster playing catch

With a crab who likes to snatch,

A swordfish in a fight
With a pirate late at night,

A puffin in a cap flying around the moon and back,

A cave on the shore
With a green seaweed door....

WANTED
Naughty SEAGULL
For stealing, spanking
and pooing in PUBLIC.
Call 7875084

The Owl and the Pussycat went to sea
In a box without very much room.
Then, hand in hand, they sailed back to land
And slept by the light of the moon,
    the moon, the moon...

And slept by the light of the moon.

for Andy, the BUMP & Amelia;
my very own naughty Seagull.
C.C.

for Jean & Gordon,
(my PARENTS).
C.R.

This edition published by
Parragon Books Ltd in 2013

Parragon Books Ltd
Chartist House
15–17 Trim Street
Bath BA1 1HA, UK
www.parragon.com

Published by arrangement with Meadowside Children's Books

Text © Coral Rumble 2013
Illustrations © Charlotte Cooke 2013
All rights reserved. No part of this publication may be reproduced, stored in a retrieval system or transmitted,
in any form or by any means, electronic, mechanical, photocopying, recording or otherwise, without the prior
permission of the copyright holder.

ISBN 978-1-4723-1988-3
Printed in China